This Little Tiger book belongs to:

Grace Fiona Swan

Love from Aunty Fee

To Thomas James, with love
~ RS
For Mum and Dad
~ GH

LITTLE TIGER PRESS
An imprint of Magi Publications
1 The Coda Centre, 189 Munster Road, London SW6 6AW
www.littletigerpress.com
This paperback edition published in 2001
First published in Great Britain 2001
Text copyright © Ragnhild Scamell 2001
Illustrations copyright © Gaby Hansen 2001
Ragnhild Scamell and Gaby Hansen have asserted their
rights to be identified as the author and illustrator of this work
under the Copyright, Designs and Patents Act, 1988.
ISBN 1 85430 755 X
5 7 9 10 8 6 4

The Wish Cat

Ragnhild Scamell

illustrated by **Gaby Hansen**

LITTLE TIGER PRESS
London

Holly's house had a cat flap.
It was a small door in the
big door so a cat could come
and go.

But Holly didn't have a cat.

One night, something magical happened. Holly saw a falling star.

As the star trailed across the sky, she made a wish.
"I wish I had a kitten," she whispered.
"A tiny cuddly kitten who could jump in and out of the cat flap."

CRASH!

Something big landed on the window sill
outside.

It wasn't a kitten . . .

It was Tom, the scruffiest, most raggedy
cat Holly had ever seen. He sat there in
the moonlight, smiling a crooked smile.

"Miao-o-ow!"

"I'm Tom, your wish cat," he seemed to say.

"It's a mistake," cried Holly.
"I wished for a kitten."
Tom didn't think Holly had
made a mistake.

He rubbed his torn ear against the window and howled so loudly it made him cough and splutter.

"Miao-o-ow, o-o-w, o-o-w!"

Holly hid under her quilt, hoping that he'd go away.

The next morning, Tom was still there, waiting for her outside the cat flap. He wanted to come in, and he had brought her a present of a smelly old piece of fish.

"Yuk!" said Holly. She picked it up and dropped it in the dustbin. Tom looked puzzled. "Bad cat," she said, shooing him away.

"Go on, go home!" said Holly, walking across to her swing.

But Tom was there before
her. He sharpened his
claws on the swing . . .

and washed his coat
noisily, pulling out bits
of fur and spitting them
everywhere.

At lunchtime, Tom sat on the
window sill, watching Holly eat.

She broke off a piece of her sandwich and
passed it out to him through the cat flap.
Tom wolfed it down, purring all the while.

In the afternoon, a cold wind swept through the garden, and Holly had to wear her jacket and scarf. Tom didn't seem to feel the cold. He followed her around . . .

chasing leaves . . .

balancing along the
top of the fence . . .

showing off.

Soon it was time for Holly to go
indoors to tea.

"Bye then, Tom," she said, and
stroked his tatty head.

Tom followed her across to the door
and settled himself by the cat flap.

That evening, it snowed.
Gleaming pompoms of
snow danced in the air.
Outside the cat flap,
Tom curled himself into a
ragged ball to keep warm.
Soon there was a white
cushion of snow all over
the doorstep, and on Tom.

Holly heard him miaowing
miserably. She ran to the
cat flap and held it open . . .

Tom came in, shaking snow all over the kitchen floor.

"Poor old Tom," said Holly.

He ate a large plate of food, and drank an even larger bowl of warm milk.

Tom purred louder than ever when Holly dried him with the kitchen towel.

Soon Tom had settled down,
snug on Holly's bed.
Holly stroked his scruffy fur,
and together they watched
the glittering stars.

Then, suddenly, another star
fell. Holly couldn't think of
a single thing to wish for.
She had everything she
wanted. And so had Tom.

More fantastic books from
Little Tiger Press

While Angels Watch

Marni McGee · Tina Macnaughton

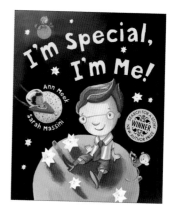

I'm special, I'm Me!

Ann Meek
Sarah Massini

ouch!

Ragnhild Scamell · Michael Terry

The Tiniest Mermaid

Laura Garnham
Illustrated by
Patricia MacCarthy

AUGUSTUS AND HIS SMILE

CATHERINE RAYNER

Bumbletum

Steve Smallman
Illustrated by
Tim Warnes

One Winter's Day

M Christina Butler
Illustrated by
Tina Macnaughton

For information regarding any of our titles or for our catalogue, please contact us:
Little Tiger Press, 1 The Coda Centre, 189 Munster Road, London SW6 6AW, UK
Tel: 020 7385 6333 • Fax: 020 7385 7333 • E-mail: info@littletiger.co.uk • www.littletigerpress.com